bindi

Wildlife Adventures

BOOK 1

TROUBLE AT THE ZOO

TROUBLE AT THE ZOO

Written by Chris Kunz

RANDOM HOUSE AUSTRALIA

A Random House book
Published by Random House Australia Pty Ltd
Level 3, 100 Pacific Highway, North Sydney NSW 2060
www.randomhouse.com.au

First published by Random House Australia in 2010

Addresses for companies within the Random House Group can be found at
www.randomhouse.com.au/offices.

National Library of Australia
Cataloguing-in-Publication Entry

Title: Trouble at the zoo / Bindi Irwin, Chris Kunz
ISBN: 978 1 86471 996 3 (pbk.).
Series: Irwin, Bindi – Bindi wildlife adventures; 1.
Target Audience: For primary school age.
Subjects: Birthday parties – Juvenile fiction
          Zoo animals – Juvenile fiction
          Water dragons (Reptiles) – Juvenile fiction
          Australia Zoo (Beerwah, Qld.) – Juvenile fiction.
Other Authors/Contributors:
          Kunz, Chris
Dewey Number: A823.4

Cover photograph © Australia Zoo
Cover and internal design by Christabella Designs
Typeset by Midland Typesetters, Australia
Printed in Australia by Griffin Press, an Accredited ISO AS/NZS 14001:2004
Environmental Management System printer.

10 9 8 7 6 5 4 3 2 1

The paper this book is printed on is certified by
the Programme for the Endorsement of Forest
Certification schemes. Griffin Press holds PEFC
chain of custody SGS-PEFC/COC-0594. PEFC
certified wood and paper products come from
environmentally appropriate, socially beneficial
and economically viable management of forests.

PEFC/COC-0594

Dear Diary,

Happy birthday to me!
I've just had the biggest and most
awesome birthday ever. Hundreds of
people were wandering around the zoo
wearing snorkels and masks – it was
hilarious! Robert had tentacles flying
everywhere and my best friend Rosie
made me this beautiful costume. We
raised heaps of money to help stop
illegal whaling. My birthday cake
was delicious and the slippery
dip was crazy fun but then
that boy Zac almost spoilt
it all by . . . Hang on, maybe
I should take a deep breath
and tell you all about it!

Bindi

CHAPTER ONE

As the sun rose on another beautiful day on the Sunshine Coast, an enormous Burmese python slithered slowly into a bedroom. In the distance, the call of the ring-tailed lemurs signalled the start of a new day. Lying asleep in bed, the young girl didn't notice the snake's progress.

Hissssssssssss. The snake took a leisurely route towards the bed, slowly winding up the bedpost until its head came to rest on the pillow. The snake's tongue flickered in and out, touching the girl's face.

The girl's face twitched a little, but her eyes remained closed. The snake let out another quiet *hissssssssssss.*

The girl's hand reached out and slowly came to rest on the head of the snake.

'Hmmm. Feels . . . scaly?' Bindi Irwin opened her eyes and smiled.

The snake smiled back.

'Have you come to wish me a happy birthday, Basil?'

Bindi's mum, Terri, and her brother, Robert, entered the bedroom, still in their PJs, and started singing. 'Happy birthday to you, happy birthday to you . . .'

Bindi jumped out of bed, super-excited. 'Yay!'

She rushed over to her mum and brother, and gave them both a big hug.

'Robert thought Basil would make a perfect birthday alarm clock,' Terri said with a smile.

'Good thinking, little buddy,' Bindi replied. 'What's for breakfast, Mum?'

'I think you might already know the answer to that, Bindi,' Terri replied.

'Woohoo, it's pancakes!' Robert and Bindi high-fived. Robert moved over to the bed to pick up Basil, who looked like he would be quite happy to snooze on Bindi's bed for the rest of the day.

'Come on, lazybones,' Robert said as he lifted the snake onto his shoulders. 'We've got pancakes to eat!'

He zoomed out of the room towards the kitchen.

Terri looked down at Bindi, and gave her a kiss on the forehead. 'Our little girl's growing up. Your dad would have loved to have been here today, sweetheart.'

Bindi gave her mum's hand a squeeze. 'I know, Mum,' she said. 'He'd have wanted it to be a fantastic day.'

'And it will be,' Terri replied, looking at her watch with a worried expression. 'Oops. As long as we get a move on!'

Bindi and Terri headed off down the hallway. 'You and Basil better have left some for us, Robert!' Bindi called out along the way.

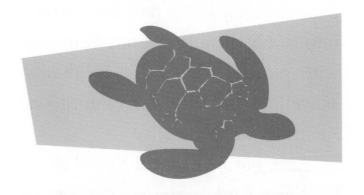

CHAPTER TWO

The Irwin family lived at Australia Zoo. They were a family dedicated to wildlife conservation. Bindi's dad, Steve, had helped change attitudes towards crocodiles with his huge enthusiasm and love for the creatures. Australia Zoo had started off as a reptile park, and they still loved their reptiles, but it had now grown into a big beautiful zoo, complete with giraffes, tigers and elephants, as well as a whole swag of gorgeous Australian animals.

After Bindi's dad had passed away, Bindi had made a promise to continue her dad's great work, alongside her family. She planned to keep that promise for the rest of her life. And her birthday was a yearly reminder of all the good that could come of passing on the message of wildlife conservation to as many people as possible.

She loved her birthday parties at Australia Zoo. This year was an underwater-themed birthday, and money earned from the day would go towards preventing whaling in Antarctica.

Bindi and Robert had just finished their last mouthfuls of delicious pancake when there was a knock at the front door.

'I'll get it,' Robert said, and ran to open the door. There on the doorstep was a very pretty mermaid. 'Ummm, Bindi, there's a mermaid here.' Robert cast a suspicious look at the mermaid and sped off down the corridor.

Bindi raced to the door. 'Oh my gosh, you look amaaaazing, Rosie!'

Rosie Bellamy was Bindi's best

friend. They had known each other since they were tiny. Rosie's dad was a vet at the Wildlife Hospital, and her mum worked at the zoo too, so Rosie and Bindi got to spend heaps of time together.

Rosie laughed. 'I wasn't sure if all the glitter was a bit much. I think I sort of scared your brother away!'

Bindi giggled. 'I promise you, Robert doesn't scare that easily.'

Rosie held up a bag. 'Happy birthday! I've got it. And it's gonna look awesome.'

Bindi squealed with excitement. 'Come on, let's go to my bedroom and try it on.'

'Okay. But don't walk too fast. Mermaids are more used to swimming than walking!'

Ten minutes later a very regal-looking emperor penguin was knocking at Bindi's bedroom door. 'Bindi, Rosie, are you ready? We've got a zoo to open!'

From behind the closed door, Terri the emperor penguin could hear giggling. 'Come on, girls . . .'

'Almost ready, Mum. Just putting the finishing touches –'

Bindi's voice dissolved into giggles once more.

A moment later, the door opened.

Rosie the mermaid stepped out, pulling the door closed behind her. 'Hi, Terri, wow, nice outfit. I have something very important to tell you: Bindi is no longer in the bedroom. Instead, I would like to introduce you to the one, the only, Stella the Seahorse!'

Rosie opened the door and a twirling, whirling vision of sparkliness made her way out of the bedroom. Bindi was dressed in a golden-coloured leotard with a layered golden skirt. The back of the leotard was draped in shimmery golden material, which looked like the frill along a seahorse's spine. She also wore a mask with a long, delicate nose. Bits of emerald green material, looking like seaweed, were strewn across Bindi's costume.

Terri was impressed. 'Wow, girls. I think this underwater-themed birthday is going to be a hit! You've made such a great costume for Bindi, Rosie.'

Rosie blushed. 'Oh, it was nothing really. You know me and Mum like sewing –'

Bindi interrupted her friend. 'It is NOT nothing. It's awesome. I love seahorses. They're such graceful and gentle creatures and this costume is the best present ever.' Bindi gave Rosie a big hug.

Terri pulled out a camera. 'Okay, girls, we've got time for a quick photo. Now hold it – one, two . . .'

'Cockatoo!' The girls struck a pose, which was interrupted a millisecond later by Robert, dressed as a blue-ringed octopus, launching himself between the two girls. Robert misjudged his jump – 'Ro-bert!' – and the two girls shrieked as all three sea creatures tumbled down in a tentacled, seaweedy heap, just as Terri took the photo.

Picture perfect – not!

CHAPTER THREE

In the car park, families were already spilling out of their cars, attaching snorkels, masks, flippers, goggles or floaties, and making their way towards the zoo entrance. There was lots of excited chatter.

Holly Brown, aged six, was

dressed up like a blue swimmer crab. She had been looking forward to coming to Bindi's birthday ever since the day she was born (so she said), and this year her dream had come true. Today also happened to be her brother's birthday, so normally she would be hanging around while her brother and his friends threw sand at each other and had competitions to see who could eat cake the fastest or who could do the biggest burp after drinking lots of fizzy drink. Yuk! She was glad she wasn't ever going to be a boy! This year Holly's mum and dad had promised her they would all go to Bindi's birthday.

Holly's brother, Zac, stood out from the rest of the excited crowd. It wasn't that he looked any different. He was wearing goggles, like plenty of other kids, and his mum was trying to slather him in sunscreen, like plenty of other kids.

The difference was that Zac Brown wore a frown.

Not one single other person, young or old, big or small, was doing anything but smiling.

Holly just couldn't understand it. She knew her brother really loved animals, especially reptiles, so even though he had been the grumpiest brother a sister had *ever* had to put up with during the car journey here, she knew he'd really enjoy being at Australia Zoo today.

It's just that to look at him, you wouldn't know.

'Hurry up, Zac. I don't want to be last in the queue to get in.' Holly was holding her mum and dad's hands, and skipping fast, making a beeline towards the entrance.

Zac was mooching behind them. 'There's no rush, okay. We'll be waiting in line forever anyway. And it's not even nine o'clock yet.'

Mr Brown, who was dressed as a sea monster and covered head to foot in seaweed, turned and gave his son one of those stern *be nice to your sister* looks, before he was dragged away.

Zac watched as a bakery van pulled up to the zoo entrance, and two delivery men manoeuvred a large birthday cake out of the van's back doors. Well, on the plus side, he did love cake, and that cake looked big enough to feed an elephant! He moved closer to the delivery men. Perhaps he could run up and sneak a taste of the icing. It looked *really* good. He inched a little closer.

Mrs Brown glanced over at her son. 'Zac, keep out of the men's way. Come over here and join the queue.'

Zac sighed as he watched the cake carried through the front entrance.

No, he did not like the way his tenth birthday was turning out, and it had only just begun.

CHAPTER FOUR

All over the zoo, staff dressed as dolphins, swordfish, slippery eels and every underwater creature you could think of were buzzing around, helping set up for the day's many activities.

Bindi, Robert and Rosie made

their way around the zoo, taking in the extraordinary sights – slippery dips and music stages were ready for action, aquamarine helium balloons were tied to signposts and enormous bubble machines were getting a test run.

A few of the zoo's employees, with walkie-talkies in hand, were busy making sure the three kids didn't see anything that would spoil the surprises the day had in store.

'Keeper one to Keeper three?' A zookeeper dressed as a puffer fish whispered into his walkie-talkie as he sped past the kids in a golf buggy. 'There's a mermaid, a seahorse and an octopus heading to the croc enclosures now. Move that cake outta there, pronto!'

Over by the crocs, a dolphin and two clown fish were moving the whale-sized birthday cake when the walkie-talkie crackled through its message. The three froze in position for a moment, and then started scampering off in the opposite direction. The clown fish kept hold of the cake while the dolphin answered the call. 'Copy that, Keeper one, or should I call you Puffer fish one? Cake taking a detour via the Tassie devils, over.'

Just past the croc enclosure, Bindi waved to a starfish setting up a popcorn stand. 'The zoo is always an amazing place,' she said to Rosie and Robert, 'but today it looks even more amazing than usual.'

'Yeah,' piped up Robert. 'Maybe everyone should dress up as underwater creatures every day.'

'That'd be cool,' said Bindi. 'Although I wonder if it would confuse the animals if their keepers began looking like animals themselves?'

Rosie pointed to a creature who was busy trimming a tree nearby. 'Is he dressed as a snail? That isn't an underwater creature, is it?'

The snail overheard the comment and turned to the kids indignantly. 'I'll have you know I'm not a garden snail, but a sea snail. Look at the stripes on my shell. I'm a Cabestana snail, of course.'

Rosie giggled. 'Well, excuse me, Mr Snail. I do apologise. I don't know as much about gastropods as I should.'

'Apology accepted,' said the snail, bowing solemnly, 'because you're such a polite mermaid. Oops, nearly forgot. Happy birthday, Bindi. You're in for a *whale* of a day.'

'Ha ha. Thanks, Mac. *Catch* ya later,' Bindi replied.

Rosie groaned. 'Oh no, the underwater jokes have started already and the zoo isn't even open yet!'

An announcement came over the PA system. It was Terri. 'Five minutes till showtime, guys. Take your starting positions. Bindi and Robert, stop "sea-horsing" around, and start running!'

The siblings rolled their eyes good-naturedly at their mother's joke. Rosie gave her friend a quick hug goodbye and raced towards the admin entrance, where she would be in charge of organising the music for the zoo opening.

A large shiny scallop shell had been placed just inside the zoo's entrance. Sparkling sand had been spread around the base of the shell and a watery blue curtain hid the scene from view.

Bindi and Robert had just reached the shell when Terri came over to join them. She gave both kids a quick hug. 'Showtime?'

Bindi had a last-minute attack of butterflies. 'I hope everything goes okay today!' she said as she glanced towards the entrance.

Terri smiled. 'Bindi Sue, we'll make sure it does!' Bindi squeezed her mum's hand and turned to Robert.

Brother and sister high-fived each other. 'Showtime,' they said in unison.

CHAPTER FIVE

'Three . . . two . . . one . . . Open those gates. Welcome, everyone, to Bindi's Eleventh Birthday Underwater Extravaganza!' From the admin office, Rosie switched off the microphone and pressed play on the CD player. A medley of underwater songs started up, the first of which was one Bindi had chosen especially for Robert and his costume – *Octopus's Garden*.

Robert and Terri were busy operating the bubble machines, and thousands of bubbles floated into the crowd. Little kids jumped and popped as many bubbles as they could.

As the guests flooded in through the gates, people were looking around. 'Where is she? Where's Bindi?'

The sea curtain was pulled away and the large scallop shell was revealed. Slowly the shell opened and Bindi the seahorse hatched out, waving and smiling at everyone.

Once the applause had died down, she welcomed the crowd. 'It's fantastic to see you all here and thank you so much for helping me celebrate my birthday today.'

Bindi loved seeing heaps of people enjoying her zoo and caring about wildlife. She was glowing with happiness as she continued her speech. 'Proceeds from today will go towards preventing whaling in Antarctica. Whales are the gentle giants of the ocean, and we just have to protect them. Earlier this year my family and I went to Antarctica, and we did see whales, but there seems to be fewer and fewer of them every year. I really believe we need to continue fighting for their survival.'

The crowd clapped in support.

Bindi continued. 'We have lots of fantastic things to see and do at the zoo today, so please enjoy yourselves. And I'll be seeing you all later on at the Crocoseum.'

The zoo staff were busy on their walkie-talkies as streams of people made their way into the zoo, and were on hand to help with any enquiries.

Robert was pumping the last bit of bubble mixture out of the bubble machine, when he decided it was time to have a go on the slippery dip. As he went to leave, a boy, who looked about ten and was wearing goggles, caught his eye. He was frowning as he walked through the entrance gates. 'Now that's not right,' thought Robert to himself. 'That boy obviously needs to laugh and he is lucky that Robert the Octopus is here to help out!'

Robert ambled over to the older boy. 'Hey there, goggle man,' he said, flicking out a few tentacles. 'What did the boy octopus say to the girl octopus?'

The boy looked slightly taken aback. Why was this octopus talking to him? 'Ummm, don't know,' he replied uncertainly.

'Can I hold your hand, hand,

hand, hand, hand, hand, hand, hand?' replied Robert, laughing at his own joke.

The boy wearing the goggles didn't even crack a smile. 'Oh, right, I get it. Eight tentacles.'

Robert was horrified. Not even a smirk? Who was this kid? Hmmm, in his experience kids who didn't have a sense of humour were trouble. He'd better keep an eye on this boy.

'Yeah, well, enjoy your day,' Robert said before racing off, his tentacles streaming behind him.

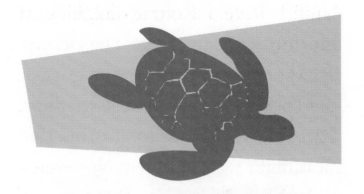

CHAPTER SIX

The slippery dip was already full of kids. Hoses squirted water onto the slides and kids propelled themselves down, screaming and laughing. Bindi and Rosie were waiting in line.

'Are you having fun, birthday girl?' Rosie asked.

'You bet,' answered Bindi. 'I can't believe everyone dressed up and looks so amazing! The photos from today will be hilarious.'

'They'll have to be better than that one your mum took of us this morning!'

Rosie had spent precious minutes rearranging sequins and chiffon after Robert's surprise entrance into the photo.

'Oh, don't remind me. I think I've got a bruise from where Robert's elbow hit me in the leg.' Bindi rubbed her shin, remembering the incident.

'Who knew octopuses had elbows?' Rosie quipped, and both girls laughed.

Bindi looked around the zoo. 'I haven't seen your parents yet, Ro,' she said. 'What costumes are they wearing?'

Rosie pointed to a pair of sea turtles over by the karaoke stage. 'They're helping with the music. Considering how much my parents love to sing, the kids will be lucky if they can get anywhere near the microphone!'

Behind the girls in the queue, Rosie noticed a boy arguing with his little sister. She looked close to tears. Rosie turned to Bindi and gave her a quiet nudge. Bindi turned around and decided to help.

'Hey there, little crab,' she said to the girl. 'What's your name?'

Holly went from miserable to thrilled in an instant. Bindi Irwin was talking to her! Holly just beamed, too excited to speak.

Zac looked at his sister, embarrassed. 'Holly, say something,' he encouraged.

'Ummm, huh, um, I'm a blue swimmer crab called Holly and it's my brother's birthday today too,' she finally blurted out.

'Oh, really. Well, what's your brother's name?' Rosie smiled at Zac. She thought he was sort of cute, even though he was wearing goggles.

Holly was getting her voice back and it was growing louder and louder by the second. 'His name's Zac, and I'm Holly, oh, I've said that already, haven't I? Ummm, happy birthday, Bindi!' She started jumping up and down.

Zac was now looking mortified. 'Calm down, Hol.'

Bindi smiled at him. 'Come on, Zac, you know what little brothers and sisters are like.' She pointed out Robert, now poised at the top of the slippery dip, about to rocket himself headfirst down the slide. 'Look at Robert up there. He's totally uncontrollable!' They couldn't help but laugh at Robert careering down, the kids on either side of him getting faces full of wayward tentacles as he flew past.

'Well, it was nice to meet you two,' Bindi smiled at the Brown kids.

Holly gave Bindi an impromptu hug and Zac looked away moodily, still wishing he was somewhere else.

Rosie rolled her eyes at his behaviour and she and Bindi got to the top of the slide, held hands and whooshed down the slippery dip, giggling all the way.

Later on, while Bindi was bringing around an eastern water dragon for people to pet, she bumped into the Brown family again.

Bindi smiled as she recognised Holly and Zac from the slippery dip. 'Hi guys. Would you like to pat the –'

Zac interrupted her, looking really enthusiastic. 'It's an eastern water dragon. I know, I love them. What's this one called?'

Bindi was a little taken aback by Zac's change of mood. 'This one's called Mardi. And she is the sweetest creature.'

'Hi, Mardi.' Zac patted the dragon carefully, with one finger along her spine. 'I've always wanted to have a lizard. I like eastern water dragons but I also really like monitors and blue tongues. Although perenties are really cool too.'

'Well, the eastern water dragons have a great life at the zoo. We have heaps of them and they get to roam freely around the place. They're really good at keeping an eye out for any leftovers that the other animals leave behind.'

Bindi turned to Holly. 'Hey Holly, keep your crab eyes on the lookout. You might see one of these beautiful girls sunning herself on our tortoises. They love the warmth of the shells and the tortoises don't seem to mind one little bit.'

Holly grinned. 'How cool.' She gave the dragon a tentative pat because, quietly, she much preferred animals covered in fur.

CHAPTER SEVEN

The sun continued to shine as the morning wore on. The animals were in good spirits. Even Agro, the zoo's grumpiest croc, seemed to be smiling today.

Staff wandered throughout the zoo, making sure everyone stayed happy and safe. 'Puffer fish one to Dolphin two, state your position, over.'

'I'm over by the fairy floss, Puffer fish one. There's been an incident, over.'

'What sort of incident, Dolphin two, over?' Starfish three was concerned and started heading towards the fairy floss stand.

Dolphin two explained. 'Nothing serious, Puffer fish one. Just a sea anemone with fairy floss stuck in her hair, over. It's almost . . .' Puffer fish one heard a yelp over the walkie-talkie as Dolphin two pulled the fairy floss out. '. . . there you go. All under control again, over.'

Puffer fish one smiled to himself, and continued scanning the crowds.

The zoo's PA system crackled. 'Attention, everyone. It's time to make your way to the Crocoseum for Bindi's birthday croc show. It starts in five minutes. You won't want to miss it.'

Holly Brown was thrilled. 'Let's go, let's go!' Her family started to move off towards the Crocoseum, but Zac lagged behind. 'Ah, Mum, Dad, I'll join you in a moment. I just . . . ahhh . . . need to go to the bathroom.'

Bindi's earlier comment about the eastern water dragons being everywhere at Australia Zoo had given Zac an idea. Perhaps his birthday was going to turn out okay after all!

'We can wait for you if you like, darling?' his mum offered.

Zac smiled sweetly. 'I'll be fine, Mum, promise. Save me a seat.' He pointed at Holly, who was almost dragging their dad towards the Crocoseum. 'You don't want Holly to miss out on the croc show.'

'Well, okay, but don't take too long,' said Mrs Brown.

Zac, still wearing his goggles,

pretended to head off in the direction of the toilet, as the crowds headed towards the Crocoseum.

If the zoo has heaps of eastern water dragons, they're not going to miss one, are they? All he'd done so far today was babysit his sister. It was time to spend some time doing what he wanted to do.

He started scanning the ground and the foliage next to the paths. He did try to keep an eye out for zoo staff, but most of them were wandering towards the Crocoseum, so he figured no-one would notice his hunting mission.

'Come on, lizards, I know you're in there somewhere . . .'

He caught a glimpse of movement out of the corner of his eye, and darted off the path into a landscaped palm garden. He tried to grab the tail of a disappearing dragon, but he wasn't quick enough.

Instead, he ended up face first in a huge mound of mulch, with a brush turkey squawking furiously at him. His goggles had fogged up during the chase, so he took them off and wiped them clean, while scowling at the brush turkey.

'Okay, okay, I'm getting off your nest. Calm down.'

The brush turkey squawked indignantly and started rebuilding his precious mound.

Zac made his way back to the path. This was only a minor setback. He was not ready to give up yet!

CHAPTER EIGHT

Robert had a few minutes free before he was needed at the bird demonstration, so he left the Crocoseum in search of a drink. The zoo was practically empty, as most of the guests were now enjoying the croc show. He was heading towards the food court when he spotted that same boy he'd seen frowning at the entrance earlier in the day. He wasn't really looking any happier and was staring pointedly at the ground. Robert had another couple of underwater-themed jokes. Maybe he could give goggle boy another go? He decided to wander over to the boy and try to make him laugh. After all, his pride was at stake!

Zac had finally spotted another dragon. He glanced around him, seeing a staff member dressed as a puffer fish off to the left picking up some rubbish. No-one was watching him. This eastern water dragon, who was a small one, about 30 centimetres long, was sunning himself on a rock just off the path, looking relaxed and happy. Zac was thrilled. This would be a proper birthday present. His very own reptile.

He picked him up gently, and stroked him. 'Hello, fella.'

Quickly, he zipped open his backpack, placed the lizard into it, and zipped it shut again. He casually glanced around him, saw no-one, and hurried towards the Crocoseum, a big grin on his face – the first one of the day.

What Zac failed to notice was the small blue-ringed octopus hiding behind a rubbish bin only a few metres from where he had stolen the reptile. Robert stood upright, flicked an angry tentacle and hurried into the Crocoseum after Zac.

CHAPTER NINE

The Crocoseum was a huge outdoor stadium where all the zoo's big animal shows were staged. There were large video screens at either end, so you could see the action taking place on stage, up close and personal. Having just finished the croc show, the zookeepers and Bindi were getting ready to start the bird demonstration. Robert raced over to his sister, and whispered something to her. She looked concerned, and Robert pointed up into the bleachers. Bindi whispered back to her brother, they both nodded seriously, and then Bindi turned on the mike.

'Well, everyone, now it's time for you to see just how clever and gorgeous our macaws are. We need a volunteer from the audience . . . You, standing up over there.' She pointed up to the bleachers. 'Please introduce yourself to the crowd. What's your name?'

Zac was up the top of the

bleachers, searching for the rest of his family, but still looking pleased with himself. He didn't realise he was the one being spoken to until everyone turned to look in his direction.

'Oh, umm, it's Zac.' He looked around, saw himself on the big video screens, and started to feel a bit uncomfortable. 'Umm, I don't really want to –'

Bindi interrupted his excuse, smiling up at him. 'Come on now, Zac, we need you. You're our parrot perch volunteer. Thanks so much.' Bindi gestured to the bird keeper, who now stood next to her, carrying a magnificent green-winged macaw.

Zac didn't know what to do. All of a sudden his good mood disappeared, and he began to think that taking an eastern water dragon and putting it in his backpack was a big mistake. You couldn't just take animals from a zoo. Could you be put in jail for doing something like that? His goggles fogged up again, this time from nervousness.

Bindi continued her speech. 'Now, here we have one of my favourite birds, Chilli the green-winged macaw. She's still in training, but let's see if she's as clever as I think she is.' Bindi leaned over and whispered something to the bird.

'Okay, Zac, put both your arms out straight, like you're making a capital T.'

Zac's breathing became shallow. He needed to calm down. He wouldn't go to jail. He was too young . . . wasn't he? Trying to stop thinking about what he'd done, he held his arms out, just as Bindi had asked.

'Okay, Chilli, do your thing!' Bindi pointed towards Zac, and the parrot took off, flying over the crowds, and landed on Zac's left arm.

The crowd burst into applause.

'Well done, Chilli. You're such a clever bird. Now, back you come,'

Bindi called out, but kept her arms at her side.

Instead of flying back, Chilli ignored Bindi's request and moved closer to the zip on Zac's backpack.

Zac looked horrified and did his best to convince the macaw to fly away. 'Hey, Chilli, fly back, fly back!'

The macaw shook her head slowly, and inched even closer to the backpack. The crowd thought the performance was wonderful.

Bindi continued trying to coerce the bird away. 'Chilli, back now, come on, I've just told everyone what a clever bird you are.'

Chilli now had the zip of Zac's backpack in her beak, and was pulling hard.

Zac wanted to faint. This was now, officially, the worst day of his life. It was his birthday, and he was going to end up in jail for stealing an animal from the best zoo he'd ever been to. How could he have been so silly?! He hoped like mad the large bird would just leave him alone, and maybe he'd get a chance to return the lizard without anyone knowing.

Bindi was looking confused. 'Gee, Zac, do you have birdseed in there? Why is Chilli so interested in your backpack?'

Zac started to reply, 'I don't know. I don't have anything in –' but was interrupted by a collective gasp of surprise, as the eastern water dragon crawled out of his open backpack and jumped onto his right shoulder.

With the macaw on one shoulder and the eastern water dragon on the other, Zac looked like a professional animal handler, and the crowd broke into applause. What a clever trick!

Bindi and Robert turned to each other, smiling, and clapped along with the audience. 'Well done, Chilli, you *are* just as clever as I thought you were.' Bindi clicked her fingers and the majestic macaw flew off

Zac's arm and back down to rest on Bindi's shoulder.

'Well, folks. As you can see, all the animals at Australia Zoo are one big happy family. They look out for one another, and I hope that you understand how important it is to respect these wonderful creatures and the habitats they live in.'

Although Bindi's speech was made to all the crowd, Zac turned a deep shade of red. He had no right to take an animal from the zoo. Not only was it stealing from the zoo, but this was the reptile's home. He felt so bad he wanted to run away right then and there, but he knew he couldn't leave without his family.

And, after all, the eastern water dragon was still happily perched on his right shoulder.

Terri the emperor penguin waddled over to Bindi the seahorse and gave her a quick hug. She turned to the crowd. 'It's now time for the cutting of the cake and –' Bindi interrupted her mum and quickly whispered something into her ear. 'Oh, okay honey.' Terri turned back to the crowd. 'Zac, the parrot perch boy up there. Bindi tells me it's your birthday too. Come on down, and you can help her cut the cake.'

Zac couldn't believe it. What was going to happen now? Was this some sort of trap? But Bindi was smiling at him, and gesturing for him to come down. She didn't look like she wanted him arrested.

Five rows down in the bleachers, Holly Brown was almost dying with excitement. 'Oh my gosh, oh my gosh, my brother's going to cut the cake with Bindi. Oh my gosh, take a photo, Mum, take a photo!'

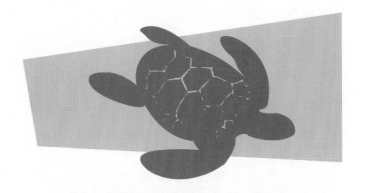

CHAPTER TEN

Kids were now queuing up to collect a piece of the birthday cake. Not only was it a whale-sized cake, it was in the shape of a whale, and there was plenty to go around. Bindi, Rosie and Zac were helping to pass out slices to the assortment of underwater creatures looking hungrily on.

One of the zoo staff had collected the dragon from Zac, looking a little surprised. 'That was a clever trick, mate. Haven't seen that one before.'

Zac opened his mouth to answer but nothing came out.

Bindi came to the rescue. 'You know we're always trying out new tricks to keep the animals entertained, Frank.'

'Well, nice work, you lot. It was a terrific show. C'mon little fella. Enough excitement for today.'

Zac watched the dragon leave. He still felt awful about what he'd done. 'Hey, Bindi, I was so totally wrong. I'm sorry,' he said quietly.

Bindi looked serious for a moment. 'It *was* a really silly thing to do, Zac. And if one of the keepers had seen what you'd done, you would've been in serious trouble.'

Zac nodded. 'I know. I wasn't thinking properly. But, tell me something, how did the parrot know the lizard was in there? Was it some kind of animal telepathy or something?'

Bindi giggled. 'Well, sort of. But it wasn't actually the parrot that knew, Zac, it was the blue-ringed octopus over there' – she pointed to her brother, who was wolfing down an enormous piece of cake, most of his tentacles already covered in chocolate and cream – 'who saw you grab the lizard in the first place.'

Zac just shook his head, ashamed.

Bindi continued. 'Look, I can tell you love reptiles like I do. And that's a great thing. Just promise me you won't do anything like that again, okay?'

'I promise.' He saw his parents making their way over with Holly, who was carefully holding onto her slice of cake. 'I better get going, I guess.'

Bindi handed him his own slice of

cake. 'Well, it's been . . . interesting meeting you, Zac.'

He smiled. 'It's been great meeting you, Bindi.' He took the cake. 'Thanks for everything.'

Holly came up to them. 'Please, please, can we both have a photo with you, Bindi?'

Zac was about to object, but he changed his mind. 'Good idea, Hol.' He gave his little sister a hug. 'Okay with you, Bindi?'

'Of course.' The three of them posed, with big smiles, each holding their slices of cake.

Mrs Brown was about to shout 'say cheese', when a small blue-ringed octopus, who had finally finished his enormous piece of cake, tripped on one of his own tentacles and went hurtling into the three of them, just as the camera flashed . . .

THE END

THE EASTERN WATER DRAGON

- The eastern water dragon is a medium to large lizard, with some specimens growing up to 80 centimetres in length.

- Eastern water dragons have large heads, with a row of spines beginning on the top of their head and leading all the way down along their back.

- They are semi-aquatic lizards that are found along the east coast of Australia, and are normally seen around creeks, rivers or lakes.

- They can remain submerged for up to 30 minutes and rise to the surface to breathe, while checking the area for danger before emerging back onto land.

- Eastern water dragons are active during both the day and night time. During this period of activity they hunt for insects, frogs, yabbies, water insects, fruit and berries.

- In the cooler times of the year, eastern water dragons will experience a dormancy period. The dragons may then dig a small hole under a log or rock, seal the entrance, and not emerge until the warmer months.

- The eastern water dragons' breeding season is in spring. Mating occurs near waterways, where the males defend their territories.

- The females lay eggs away from the river in moist soil nests. Female dragons can lay 10-20 eggs.

ANIMAL FACT FILE

THE GREEN-WINGED MACAW

- Green-winged macaws grow to lengths of up to 90 centimetres and have a wingspan of up to 1.2 metres.

- They have a large curved beak that is used for cracking nuts and acts as an aid in climbing.

- Macaws also have the zygodactyl foot configuration with two middle toes facing forward and the two outside toes facing backward. This helps them to hold food and climb.

- The green-winged macaw is a deep shade of red, with dark green on the wings.

- Their faces are lined with deep-red feathers, while their flight feathers are blue. Their tail feathers are blue with a red tip and are shorter than other macaws within the same family.

- Macaws can be found in forests, swamplands, open savannahs, palm groves and along riverbanks in much of South America, ranging from Panama to Paraguay and east to the Guianas and Trinidad, and south to Argentina.

- The green-winged macaw's diet consists of seeds, fruits, nuts and limited vegetable matter.

- They have regular roost sites for the evenings and in the early mornings they will fly to their feeding grounds.

- Macaws create nests in holes near the tops of trees. Usually two eggs are laid by the female with an incubation period of 24 to 26 days.

- The young are fledged in 13 weeks and reach adulthood in six months.

Become a
Wildlife Warrior!

Find out how at
www.wildlifewarriors.org.au

If you'd like to find out
more about stopping
whaling in Antarctica,
Bindi and Australia Zoo
recommend visiting
www.seashepherd.org.